About the Author

David Kitchen is an entrepreneur and businessman, running a group of consultancy companies that work with and support SME businesses. He sits on the board of several high growth companies as a Non-Executive Director, providing advice and guidance to Directors as a specialist in business growth and mergers & acquisitions. He has always wanted to write, and this, his first book was written in 2022 in Spain, the first time he had specifically put aside enough time to focus on his writing.

Second Time Around

David Kitchen

Second Time Around

Olympia Publishers
London

www.olympiapublishers.com
OLYMPIA PAPERBACK EDITION

Copyright © David Kitchen 2024

The right of David Kitchen to be identified as author of
this work has been asserted in accordance with sections 77 and 78 of
the Copyright, Designs and Patents Act 1988.

All Rights Reserved

No reproduction, copy or transmission of this publication
may be made without written permission.
No paragraph of this publication may be reproduced,
copied or transmitted save with the written permission of the publisher,
or in accordance with the provisions
of the Copyright Act 1956 (as amended).

Any person who commits any unauthorised act in relation to
this publication may be liable to criminal
prosecution and civil claims for damage.

A CIP catalogue record for this title is
available from the British Library.

ISBN: 978-1-80439-905-7

This is a work of fiction.
Names, characters, places and incidents originate from the writer's
imagination. Any resemblance to actual persons, living or dead, is
purely coincidental.

First Published in 2024

Olympia Publishers
Tallis House
2 Tallis Street
London
EC4Y 0AB

Printed in Great Britain

Dedication

This book is dedicated to my partner Tracy and son Alex, who allowed me the time and space to be able to concentrate on my first book, thank you!

Chapter One – Success

Cobham, Surrey, August 2018

Driving home from a successful day at the office, Mike Stead was a man on top of the world. A deal done today that should pay for his Caribbean month away next year – and the rest. Life is good and he is grateful for the things and the people he has in his life.

As he pulls into the drive in his new Black S-Class Mercedes he can see his wife Debbie through the kitchen window. The mother of his two children, Kenny (8) and Louisa (6) she is as beautiful today as the very first time he set eyes on her. With sparkling blue eyes, blonde hair and a figure to die for she always looks stunning – even with no make-up, which she never wears – plus her positive and fizzy personality to match.

As he walks through the door, all descend on Mike including Harvey the dopey Springer Spaniel who climbs all over him. "Dad, I got picked for the school football team" said Louisa whilst Kenny simultaneously said something about girls not being able to play football.

Debbie smiled, "How was your day, darling?"

"Great," said Mike, "we got the Bellingham deal done, so it's time to book the Caribbean!" and they all cheered.

Mike is the owner and Director of a commercial loan brokerage – Stead Commercial – based in Guildford, finding the right lender to place companies for either new or refinancing deals. Mike employs twelve staff who all have some involvement in the deals they handle. Bellingham's were a new client that he had spent the Spring months working on himself and the money had been released today. James Bellingham the owner was really grateful and had asked Mike if they wanted to join them in a charity project together – a day care centre for children with physical and mental disabilities and Mike was feeling like it would be good to give something back.

As they all sat down to dinner – Harvey included – they all groaned as Theresa May came on their screens and it was all about Brexit once again!

Chapter 2 – Career Move

Warrington, November 1999

Dave Lawrence could not believe his luck and it was all real now. As the plane started its descent into JFK airport, he could see the lights of New York below. For an ordinary lad who had grown up in Warrington, Cheshire it seemed like a dream for a local to be chosen for a three-year placement in New York.

He had started with RBS in the Warrington branch in 1995 as a twenty-two-year-old graduate. Admittedly he was bright, had always excelled in school, gained good results and he was admitted to the bank on a fast-track trainee management programme. The first year or so had been utterly dull, working in a branch, on the counter, doing the admin behind the counter and other endless, tedious tasks. Things looked up when he was transferred to the business centre, and he enjoyed working in the foreign currency department. It was when he started to get into trading and derivatives that things got interesting – the bets, gambles, well thought out investments and all other types of rolling the dice were a real eye opener and he started to excel in dealing with customers and winning new investment opportunities for the bank.

When he was called into the Director's office in August, he had no idea what was coming. Edward Riley was a bit stuffy, old school, wearing his old tatty suit and his bank tie and he took a long time to get to the point. The short version was that they were really pleased with Dave's work, he was an absolute natural, would go far in the bank and that they had decided to send him on secondment to the New York office to learn more about international business banking with a view to him coming back and taking over from Riley when he retires in 3 ½ years' time.

It had been a whirlwind few months since that day and sad saying goodbye to his mates in Warrington – and Manchester where he was now based. He was very upset at having to say goodbye to his dad, who is really not very well. After Dave's mum died in 1990, Dad never really recovered from the shock of her cancer and became a bit reclusive, over reliant on the booze at home and got very old and very Ill all rather quickly. At fifty years old, with just a part time job at a local factory he looked much older than his years and his lungs sounded like they were giving up as a result of the forty per day he still smoked.

Dave had been devastated by his mum's death. She was such a vibrant, outgoing woman so full of fun and laughter. It all happened within about three months when she went to the hospital with a sharp pain in her head, which turned out to be a tumour. They attended her funeral only twelve weeks later. With no other brothers or sisters Dave grew apart from his dad as they went on different trajectories, Dave focusing on his work, exams, results and then his newly found employment at the bank.

The flight landed on time and Dave was bursting at the seams to see the city that never sleeps and looking forward to making new friends in the Big Apple

Chapter 3 – New Life

New York, February 2000

New York was everything Dave wanted and expected. The job was great – working with some amazing traders in the lower levels of the South tower of the World Trade Centre and out every night, them generously spending their bonuses on him, he was having a party time. His work was more about organisation, project management and systems, supporting the day traders who made millions of dollars for the bank.

He had recently met Melissa who had shown lots of interest in her 'cute' Englishman friend, and they had now started dating properly. Melissa worked in a creative design studio in Brooklyn, she had lots of friends, attended lots of parties and had the life of a real New York party girl but for some reason she had decided it was the dark good looks and trim body of the Cheshire lad she wanted spend her time with. Her dad worked with the Trump organisation and seemingly earned a fortune – they had a sprawling ranch 10 miles outside the city.

Melissa wanted an apartment overlooking Central Park and she was always trying to get Dave to come looking. In the end he agreed, worried about the cost, of course but he was getting the idea that whatever Melissa wanted she got.

They signed up for a wonderful two bed apartment overlooking Central Park which was dreamland for Dave as well as Melissa. Riding on the crest of a wave, they married only six weeks later, and he was completely in love with his new bride, but the worry over the costs of their lifestyle were nagging away at the back of his mind.

They lay in bed the day after their wedding which took place in the Refinery Hotel, a former hat factory now a fabulous luxury hotel with magnificent views over the city. Melissa's dad Frank had paid for the wedding, attended by only twenty-five guests but a fortune none the less. Dave had a couple of his new friends from work but of course his dad couldn't make it – he sounded closer to death than ever and there was a guilt factor of course for Dave as he lived the high life in New York.

"What plans do you have for the future Melissa?" asked Dave looking up at the Georgian artwork on the bedroom ceiling.

"I want to have sex with you every day Dave, own my own studio, travel across Europe and buy a ranch the size of mum and dads, how's that for starters?" she said.

Dave laughed, rolled on top of her and said, "OK let's make a start," and made love to her for the umpteenth time that night/morning.

They looked out at the Empire State Building and marvelled at the city which must be the best city in the world, they both agreed.

Chapter 4 – Job Interview

Guildford, April 2004

Mike put on his best shirt and tie. He had spent the best part of two years working as an assessor for a training company which was very relaxed, t-shirt and jeans. The learners were mostly unemployed trying to get back into employment, government sponsored. Suit, shirt and tie would be too much for those learners who would find it a bit intimidating.

Today was a bit different – an interview with Joe Radford, owner of Guildford finance brokers, a long established and well-respected brokerage going back to the late 1960s, started by Joe's now deceased father William Radford.

Mike really wanted the job. The assessing role was very dull even though it was genuinely helping people back to work and satisfying. His real interest was in finance and commercial lending/broking was exactly what he wanted to do.

Joe was a lovely guy, a real gentleman, old fashioned in that you rarely meet people with the manners, politeness and respect that this man extended to you. Joe asked some testing questions of Mike, but he answered as honestly as possible, showing some vulnerability and Joe offered him the job there and then with a handshake that spoke a thousand words.

Mike was delighted and went to his local the Rose and Crown in Wokingham and sank a few pints at the bar in celebration. He had a few fellow drinkers that he often spoke with and shared stories, but it would be an exaggeration to suggest they were friends. All lonely boozers who shared a common interest. He proudly told each and every one of his 'mates' about his new job.

The following Monday Mike started work and spent ½ day with Joe and his number two Andy who was a Mr nice guy, jolly, friendly, always looking to help people and with arm round the shoulder. There seemed to be no edge or agenda with Andy, and everyone loved him to bits.

Mike loved the job and was fantastic with the clients. He built some really good relationships with many of the businesses and Joe soon made him Senior Client Relationship Manager. Around six months after joining he was working with Priestley Engineering in Newbury, a £10m manufacturer of Aluminium Windows and Curtain Walling. On his second visit to Newbury, he noticed a stunning blonde girl in the admin offices who took his breath away. Debbie Jeffries was the niece of Neil Priestley the MD and was working as family support in HR and Finance to the Directors. "Hi," said Mike, "I saw you last time I was here, how's it going?"

"Fine," said Debbie, "so much better for seeing you again. "That was the start of a wonderful relationship and after spending nearly every day together after that, they married two years later."

Chapter 5 – The Honeymoon is Over

New York, January 2001

The shine had gone off Dave and Melissa's golden relationship already. Melissa continued to want more and more, Dave struggled to live up to her father's granting of her every wish, and he had been accumulating more and more debt to pay for her every want and need. As well as the super expensive apartment overlooking Central Park, Melissa had set her heart on a brand-new BMW convertible and Dave would be on the wrong end of her disappointment if he didn't provide it for her.

He started to get very worried about the level of debt he was getting into after the new bedroom refurbishment. He couldn't speak to her about it because she was so used to getting her own way and her dad buying everything for her that she would have been disgusted at the idea he had got into debt to pay for what she considered to be reasonable and everyday items.

Dave finally confided in a friend – Sean Delaney who he often met after work in O'Hara's bar in Cedar Street. They had initially spoken after a policeman had got drunk in the bar and started smashing the place up – an open-mouthed moment for most. The policeman was subsequently arrested and dismissed from NYPD. "What the freaking heck was that?" said Sean as they both burst out laughing and a friendship was born.

Dave told him about Melissa, how she had become more distant, spending more and more time out with her friends, staying out late sometimes until morning and expecting him to provide more 'things', getting frostier and more unfriendly if he questioned it.

Sean's family owned the Shamrock Construction Company, one of New York's major construction businesses currently embedded in some of the city's major developments. Sean said he would speak to his cousin Ger who was a Director of the organisation who may be able to help with refinancing. Dave really appreciated it.

In May that year he was called in front of the RBS Director and HR representative on the 8th floor who gave him a severe dressing down about his debts. "As an employee of the bank you know that you should not get into debt. We need to be above criticism in terms of our personal finances, and you were aware of that when you joined the bank. We conduct annual reviews of all staff and we have discovered that you have what appears to be around $100,000 of debt, far beyond any reasonable amount for someone at your level in the organisation. We are putting you on notice that unless we can see this being greatly reduced in the next three months, we will have to terminate your employment."

That was a stunner and another real worry in his life. He had always been so good at his job and loved it – he was now in danger of losing his employment, what would he tell Melissa?

To make matters worse Dave's dad died a week after the warning he received from RBS. Dave travelled back to Warrington for the funeral, there were only four people there, he quickly got things dealt with and came back to New York. His dad lived in a rented house and left nothing.

In late June he finally managed to meet up with Ger in his prestigious offices on Fifth Avenue where his part of the Shamrock organisation was based. To his credit Sean also turned up and made a personal introduction and recommendation for Dave and after a jovial chat about the merits of Rugby League over Rugby Union, Sean said his goodbyes.

Ger explained the history of the organisation, how their family had migrated in the early 1900s from Cork to New York and despite the early hardship they had now grown a billion-dollar organisation with property interests across the US. He admitted they are very cash rich and often provide loans to individuals and companies where they are suffering hardship. "Not often to bank employees admittedly," he laughed.

Dave told his story, admitted he had been very foolish in allowing Melissa to behave the way she had and in getting into debt, but he needed the job and to find a way out of this predicament he had got himself into. Amazingly Ger said that they would pay off his $100k debts if he showed him all the statements and would ask for an initial $2,000 per month repayment, increasing when he could afford it and got promoted. It was not like getting a loan from a bank, very relaxed and trusting.

They agreed to meet next week – early July, with all his statements and get it done. As it turned out Ger had to fly to San Francisco to close a deal, so they actually met up towards the end of July. Ger was true to his word and settled all the debts there and then by direct bank transfer. As they shook hands and he walked out Ger said, "Oh and by the way I might need you to give me an introduction to a couple of the best traders over at the bank, if that's OK?" Yes, no problem said Dave who thought that was just reciprocal business and didn't recognise that the

$100,000 was not the only debt he now owed Ger; he had also not realised that this moneylending was off the books of Shamrock and in fact a money laundering scam.

When he got home that afternoon (he had taken the day off work to get the deal done with Ger) he went home early, feeling fantastic and that all his problems were solved, and he could keep his job as his credit rating would now be repaired. As he opened the door of the apartment, he heard the unmistakeable noise of Melissa and her loud sex groans. His heart nearly stopped as he heard her enjoying someone else's body as she had so many times enjoyed his. He felt sick, retreated from the hallway and went out. He was devastated, after all the debt he had run up and everything he had done to try and please her, she had been cheating on him all that time. He had suspected as much but could not face it. He now had to face it and after a trip to O'Hare's for the afternoon to drown his sorrows he decided it was now time for a change – and he would now make a plan.

Chapter 6 – Credit Crunch

Guildford, August 2008

It was a Wednesday afternoon when the reality hit. The news had been circulating for weeks and it had been clear the banks were stopping lending, but no one thought that the "credit crunch" was the biggest financial catastrophe in a century.

Joe gathered his team around and through the tears in his eyes said "ladies and gentlemen I'm afraid I have bad news. The trauma in financial markets in the US has spread to here. The supply of money has completely dried up and we are not going to be able to continue to do business. We cannot arrange and supply loans when there is no money to lend and therefore our income has stopped indefinitely. I have no choice but to close down the business. I am really sorry folks this is very painful for me, you have all been fantastic to work with and you have helped us be the best in class in this market, but it is over. We still have some cash reserves in the business and have worked out that we can pay you all three months wages, which hopefully will tide you over until you get a new job. Once again, I am so sorry" and he tailed off as tears started streaming down his face. Like everyone else Mike was truly shocked as he did not expect this turmoil in US markets would affect his fantastic job here in Guildford, but in a global economy everyone is affected wherever they are.

Mike went home to his and Debbie's house in Woking. Debbie now worked in admin for the NHS after the family firm in Newbury was bought out by a large conglomerate. She was therefore lacking knowledge of the impending financial doom and it was a great shock to her that Mike was now out of work. The three months' notice was such a generous gift by Joe and would help them immensely in this difficult time and they were grateful of that. Debbie knew that their wish to start a family would have to wait and she felt her own time bomb ticking away inside her as she now approached thirty.

In fact, the "credit crunch" was bigger than everyone thought and when Lehman Brothers fell in September 2008 the impact on the US and UK economy was significant.

Mike applied for lots of jobs but there seemed to be nothing doing. He re-approached the training company to see if there were any assessor roles going and as the number of unemployed had now risen again, this was probably his best bet. He was on the way to the interview in Croydon when he got a call from Peter Rose, CEO of Harland Chemicals in Tyneside who said, "Hello, Mike, you know that refinancing deal we were doing with you earlier in the year which we had to put on hold because of the potential acquisition? Well, the acquisition has fallen through so we have decided to go for the refinancing deal – is it still on?" Mike explained that he was no longer part of Guildford finance brokers as they had closed down. "I appreciate that Mike, but you were the person I dealt with, we got along very well and I know you did a great job in finding us the right deal – I want to deal with you – can you do it for us?" Mike said he would love to and would come back to Peter within the next two days.

Of course, it would not be easy as the market had shredded, but he had got to find a way. He didn't have a Consumer Credit

Licence so couldn't get the finance and commission as a broker so he would need to find a way to do it somehow. He would also need to find a lender who could refinance £5m, although in his favour Harland were a great credit risk.

Mike stalled the training company and called every lender he knew. On the 24th call he seemed to get lucky as his contact there referred him to a private equity firm who they knew were looking to invest in traditional and manufacturing type businesses. He called the owner Rupert Woodhead and had a great chat with him, and it looked like there may be some mileage in it.

Mike drew up two contracts, similar to that of Joe's but as more of an informal introducer and consultant. The contract stipulated that Harland would pay Mike three per cent of any successful funds raised at the point of completion. He called Peter, submitted his contract and Peter was happy to sign as it was 1.5 per cent less than the brokerage were going to charge. For Mike it could be a real life changer.

Mike spent the next nine days preparing all of the submissions and documents that Rupert needed, liaising with Peters PA, and also calling more lenders. He found a small lender in Edinburgh who would consider the case and he put it together for them too.

Once all that was done, he reluctantly accepted that he had to go and earn a living and took a job with the training company to help people stop being unemployed which was ironic.

As it turned out both the PE firm and the lender offered Harland the £5m refinancing and Peter accepted the loan instead of the equity. The deal completed in March 2009 and actually surprised Mike as he was embroiled in his day job; to say he had forgotten about the deal would be wrong, but it had been filed away for another day. When he got the call, he was delighted and went home to celebrate with Debbie. They went away to Dublin for the weekend, staying at the Clayton Hotel overlooking the Liffey and it was one of the best weekends they ever spent together. They made plans for their future life, which involved Mike using the money to set up his own brokerage business and the two of them making several miniature Mike and Debbie's.

Chapter 7 – Bank Shock

New York, September 2001

Dave's plan was to ask the bank to reassign his secondment to their base in California for the second half of his assignment. He said that he really wanted to understand new banking with tech companies and working in Silicon Valley would be great personal development. He also told his manager in New York about his marriage split from Melissa (not that she knew yet – he had more courage to tell the bank than he did her!). He provided evidence of the £100k debts now paid off and said it was from his father's estate who died recently.

As it turns out the bank said no to the transfer and still intended to continue the disciplinary process for his debt situation as Dave couldn't evidence the actual money received from the will. His disciplinary hearing was set for 18 September, and he was gutted, he thought he had done enough and also had a good case for the transfer. His manager had seemed to understand and been sympathetic, but it seemed HR had refused it. He was now in grave danger of losing his job.

Dave's plan was now to 'do a runner.' He had no reason to stay in NY, he owed Shamrock $100k, he had a cheating wife who he now saw as the good time girl that she is, and he is going to lose his job. He therefore decided to go back to each of his credit cards, withdraw as much cash as he could, buy a van (he purchased a van from a dealer in Philadelphia) and make his way across America to the West Coast and start a new life for himself. He would keep a low profile, operate in cash and hopefully disappear under the radar of his creditors.

Over the course of five days, he systematically drew out cash from the banks and managed to accumulate around $50,000. He had also gone to Teds tattoo parlour where he knew (Sean had explained to him) Ted used the tattoo business as a front and he created false documents, driving licences and passports and was very discreet.

On that particular Tuesday morning, he was slightly late for work as he had gone to collect his new passport before he picked up a few things from his office (such as his old passport) and then he was away on his new adventure.

As he made his way to the South Tower, he couldn't believe his eyes as a plane flew into what looked like the top of the North Tower. Everyone looked up, were completely shocked, some screamed, some ran, others stood still in shock. How could a plane misjudge its path and fly into a building, it was madness. Dave was still focused on his task despite being in shock personally as he saw the fire spread across the whole building. He still headed towards his office and when only one block away the most incredible thing happened – a second plane hit his own workplace building at the same height – it was sabotage not an accident!

That was enough for Dave and all others in the area to run – the opposite way – and head away from the towers. There was smoke, noise, shouting and sheer panic as people now realised what this was. Dave felt like he was in some sort of dream – well, nightmare – and he couldn't think straight. He just kept running. Not really conscious of which direction and how far, he ran past Soho, Lower Manhattan and Washington Park before he eventually saw a cheapish looking hotel – The Central Hotel on 7th Avenue, fairly close to the opposite side of Central Park to where he lived.

He went inside and asked for a room. The server never looked at him, watching his TV screen constantly as the pictures were beamed round the world – it was a terrorist attack! America was being attacked, who would have believed it? Dave went to his small, seedy room, laid on the bed and switched on the TV to see the story unfolding, not only in New York but the Pentagon too.

Had there ever been a day like this before?

Dave stayed in the hotel for a couple of days – he only went out to buy food which he brought back to his room. He disguised himself slightly as he did not want to be recognised. He realised that his last trip to work had been to pick up his British passport which sat in his office. His plan to "do a runner" had taken another twist now as people would probably expect that he had been killed at work as the Towers were destroyed. If any remnants of his passport were left that would provide some sort of evidence of his death. Little did Dave know, even twenty years on from the Twin Towers terrorist attack over 1,000 victims had yet to be identified.

Several days after checking in Dave made his way to the Port Authority Bus Terminal (PABT) and took the eight-thirty a.m. bus to Philadelphia. Once there he walked the 3 miles to the dealer who he had purchased the camper van. There were no problems and he set off on his journey of a new life and freedom.

Over the coming months Dave made his way, posing as an Australian on a long vacation across Pennsylvania, Ohio, Indiana, Illinois, Missouri and Dallas before deciding to stay and spend time in Albuquerque, New Mexico. He enjoyed his early freedom on the road and stopped off many times during the 2000-mile journey making acquaintances but not friends. He did not want to give any clue as to his true identity and made sure he kept his distance.

In Albuquerque he got some lodgings and worked in a sports bar for a couple of months which he really enjoyed until he was severely beaten up by two dodgy looking customers from the bar who he had never seen before but clearly, they had set eyes on him. He was leaving the bar at one a.m. as they jumped out on him in the side street – the back entrance to the bar – and took the $50 he had on him. Luckily his flat and car key were kept in the key lock facility next to his front door.

It was so senseless; they didn't seem to want anything other than whatever money he had, and they gave him a good beating – kicking his ribs and legs and creating severe bruising. Again, wanting to protect his identity he let the bar owner know he was ill and laid low for a few days before getting back in the camper van and heading for Los Angeles. It was another 1,000 miles, but he had decided that now – six months on from the Twin Towers attack, and his exit from New York, perhaps it was time to return to his native England. The beating up had affected him badly and he decided that staying in the US was not what he wanted to do.

He had been careful with the money and now with it he purchased a one-way flight to London Heathrow from LAX. He flew in April 2002 and whilst he was still nervous about his identity and being 'found out' part of him felt like he was heading for home.

Chapter 8 – Charity Work

Guildford, November 2018

Mike shook the hands of each of the members of staff who worked for the day centre. He and James Bellingham had laid on a real treat for the staff, parents and kids with a big celebratory meal and some new equipment for the centre. Some new computers, virtual reality sets and video games were all installed in the new 'tech room' which was an absolute delight for all concerned.

Afterwards Mike and James walked across to the Golden Lion where they sat and had a few beers. They had become friends as well as working partners and this charity event had been the culmination of several months planning and working together. A reporter from the Surrey Advertiser who had been covering the event quite discreetly, entered the bar and made a beeline for the two men.

"Hi, Mike. Hi, James, that was quite some event."

"Yes, it certainly was," said James, "it is so good to see those kids faces playing on those VR kits."

After a little small talk, the three of them went their separate ways.

Four days later Mike was walking across from his office to his regular coffee shop haunt, Kofi's. He was not sure whether it was named after the former secretary general of the UN Kofi Annan – he had never asked – but he certainly felt peace when he went in there most days. He always sat in a certain booth just away from the front window where he could think and take notes on his iPad. In Mike's mind having time to think, review and plan was important as a businessman.

After a few minutes a strange but familiar face appeared in front of him as the tall man sat down. "Hi Dave, it's been a long time – I saw your picture in the paper – the charity event – what on earth are you doing using our old mate's name?"

"Sorry," said Mike, "I'm Mike Stead, there must be some mistake."

"Dave, we went to Penketh High together, we played in the school football team together, we went to Live Aid together with my mum and dad, who do you think you are fooling," said Andy Thompson, his old school mate.

Chapter 9 – Beware the Railway Line

Warrington, September 1981

We used to play over the railway wall. Picking and eating elderberries, playing hide and seek, building dens and kissing girls (whilst playing hide and seek) – we were too young I know but it didn't seem like it at the time.

We were playing over the wall on the final day before we went back to school. It was next to the bridge so the people walking onto the bridge at the other side could see us from there. We saw 'Piggy' Parkin walking towards the bridge. We are never sure when the animosity started between us and Piggy Parkin and his mates, but I think it was over some firewood for bonfire night. On one occasion we had chanted his slang name – foolishly, as he was bigger, stronger and older than any of us and he looked a real bruiser. Every time we saw him, we ran.

Parkin saw us on the bank and started to run across the bridge. We panicked as always, and I ran down the path behind the railway wall behind the houses in our street. I was conscious that the others had gone in a different direction but at the point of fleeing you just run. Seconds later I heard a screech as the brakes of the train tried to slow as they collided with an eight-year-old boy. We always made sure we never ran across the tracks but on this occasion, Michael was obviously so scared he just ran across to the other bank and forgot to look for trains.

On the 5 of September 1981 Mike Stead was killed by a train.

Almost twenty years to the day later, Dave Lawrence – wanting to escape his own life and create a new identity, used the 'legend' of Mike, firstly getting a false passport in his name and later, when back in the UK getting a copy of his birth certificate, then driving licence, bank accounts and the rest.

Mike (Dave) had almost forgotten himself that he was someone else and perhaps his defences had slipped as he had done the charity event and allowed reporters to take photos.

Chapter 10 – Sharing His Story

Guildford, 2018

Andy had seen the picture in the newspaper of the charity event. Even though much older he recognised his old school friend. In truth Andy was much keener on his friend back then than the other way round and Dave (Mike) was still in his thoughts to this day. When he saw the name Mike Stead, he did a double take as he would never forget the day that his young pal walked onto the railway line. Andy was there on the day, and he remembers his own father driving up the street in his police car desperate to find out that it wasn't Andy that had been killed. The news that an eight-year-old lad had been killed in their street was enough to bring tears as he drove all the way back; when he saw Andy, he was so relieved the tears of anguish were replaced by tears of relief as he hugged his young lad.

Mike told Andy the whole story, going to New York with the bank, Melissa, the money problems and how he was close to the scene of 9/11 just as he had decided to change his identity and escape his creditors.

As he always had been Andy was a good listener, sympathetic and a good friend, promising never to tell anyone and to keep it as their secret. In return Andy updated him on his life, how he had been in the building industry and now got his own building firm in partnership with another friend. He still lived in the Northwest but was often down in leafy Surrey as most of the prestigious building jobs were down here, so he spent a great deal of time in hotels.

Mike asked about Andy's brother who had been a troublemaker at school. "Sadly, he was arrested a few times as a teenager and things went from bad to worse; he is living a life of crime – doing well out of it but he's been inside a couple of times. He is out at the moment and spends most of his time at the Clayton end with the Stanley Ultras at Accrington Stanley," they both laughed although neither really knew why.

A friendship had been re-born and Andy was keen to continue to stay close to his old friend. Mike on the other hand wanted to keep his distance. This was the first time his big secret had come out and he was pretty shocked that it had; he had to keep a lid on it and make sure this did not get out any further and the more he could stay out of Andy's way the better he thought.

They shook hands, then hugged and both vowed to see each other again soon, Andy promised once again that Mike's secret would stay that way.

Mike went home after that, shocked to the core that someone knew. It was a slight relief in one way to have spoken to someone from his old life – he used to think about them a lot in his early days as Mike but latterly the love for his wife and children were enough to take up all of his thoughts and energy and he could not bear the thought of any of that being lost.

Chapter 11 – An Ugly Encounter

Guildford, September 2019

Business still good, Mike was in Kofi's as usual at ten-thirty a.m., working out the structure of a new deal with a new client he had been speaking to since eight a.m. this morning. It was a management buyout of a solicitor's practice, where the new partners had plenty of cash, but the firm was making such a huge profit the exiting partner needed more, so a finance deal was being arranged.

As his pen drew the numbers a face appeared at his booth, in a similar way to the way Andy had done last year. "Mind if I sit here?" said the big man with tattoos on his neck, a tooth missing and evil eyes.

"Do I know you?" asked Mike.

"I'm Karl, Andy's business partner and one night when we got thoroughly pissed, he spilled your story. He even told me how to find you. He's a dick and we are not in business any more. Now I hear you have quite a story that you don't want people to find out?"

"Sorry Karl I don't know what you mean," said Mike.

"Don't give me that fuckin' shit mate or I will beat the fuck out of you. Let's not mess about, I know about New York, the moneylenders, your dead mate on the railway track and your false little cosy life here with your business – which looks like it's doing pretty well – and your nice big house worth about two

Mill – so let's not beat about the bush. I want fifty grand by Friday, and you'll never see me again, otherwise you and your lovely wife will have iron bar marks in the back of your skull and the world will know about your story – got it?"

"How do I know you won't come back for more or tell the story anyway?"

"You don't sunshine, now get me the fifty grand and I'll see you in here on Friday same time," and with that Karl left as suddenly as he had appeared.

Mike was shell-shocked – his whole world was potentially about to come down around him. He could get £50k – he had money in his savings account and many nil balance credit cards. But of course, the worry is he just keeps coming back and/or he publicises what he clearly knows to the world at large.

Mike drove out in his car to Bracknell Forest. He needed time to think, and he didn't have much time. He decided to call Andy and ask him about Karl.

"Hi, Andy, how are you?"

"Not so good Mike, I realise I went into business with the wrong person – he not only cheated me and took the money out of our accounts but also had me done over by some of his gangland mates. I am in a bad way, still in bed and feeling very sorry for myself. Oh, I guess he has been to see you?"

"Yes, Andy he is threatening me for money and with violence and tell all unless I pay up. Do you think he will come back for more if I pay him?"

"Yes, Dave… er Mike I am sure he will. He is a very nasty piece of work and I found out the hard way once we had done a few jobs and got money into the company – there is no easy way out for you, especially as you need to keep it all secret."

"Why did you tell him Andy, you promised...?"

"Oh, Mike I am so sorry, I think he spiked my drink and I spilled everything about everyone, I cannot apologise enough."

"Do you have his phone number," asked Mike and Andy told him the number.

Later that night Mike went for a walk down the street and called Karl. "Look Karl, I will get you the £50k but I need an extra couple of days. I am coming to Birmingham on Monday lunchtime so to save you coming down here I could meet you at Birmingham New Street station instead around one p.m.?" Karl was silent for a minute and then agreed. After all it was worth it for his £50k bonus payday.

Mike went to work on his plan and made his way up to Birmingham on Saturday and Sunday via Cambridge and Peterborough by train, getting the nine fifty-four from Platform 7 at Peterborough into New Street for eleven forty-five. He had met people in Cambridge and Peterborough and felt adequately equipped to deal with Karl when he saw him.

Mike went onto the top floor of New Street station, now 'Grand Central' – a whole lot better than the old Bullring of the past. He went to Café Concerto where you could view all of the ground floor area, passengers coming and going – and more importantly Pret-A-Manger, where he watched and waited for his new enemy Karl to arrive, whilst consuming a coffee and cake. Mike was disguised with a bald head covering, thick glasses and a false beard. He had a walking stick and with a bent posture he looked twenty years older than his true years.

At last, he saw Karl arrive – on his own thankfully – and he sat in a seat in Pret with his back to the general flow of people traffic. Mike made his way slowly down the escalator and limped towards Pret and to the rear of Karl. As he got close his gloved hands took the needle from his safety wallet and whilst appearing to stumble slightly, he pushed the needle into the back of Karl's neck.

Karl's head dropped but he stayed in an upright position, not alerting other coffee shop customers. The needle contained a deadly cyanide mix he had purchased from a new contact he gained on the dark web last week. He had been careful to hide his identity and appearance and kept the substance well protected as he stayed in his Peterborough B&B.

The effect of the stabbing was pretty instant as Karl died within seconds. Mike, looking like a very old man who had stumbled continued to walk towards the lift where he descended onto the platform. He was away from the scene within a few seconds and before the Pret staff or customers noticed that Karl had passed away.

In the lift – alone of course – he removed his coat, beard, bald covering and he retracted the stick to the size of an umbrella and put them all in his reversable hold all (which was now bright red instead of black), completely changing the appearance of the old man who walked past the coffee shop only minutes beforehand.

Mike didn't know whether the dose would be enough to kill Karl but the research he had done and the many conversations he had with the dodgy people he bought the cyanide mix from, gave him enough comfort that it would work.

It didn't hit Mike until he arrived at his next destination (Cheltenham) that he had killed a man. That night he tossed and turned and went through a huge range of emotions – firstly not knowing whether Karl was dead, but also the potential of him having taken a person's life which is something he could never have imagined himself doing.

He continued his long-winded journey back to Surrey via Bristol, and Paddington over the next two days, scouring the newspapers before eventually seeing that the Birmingham Mail confirmed that a man had died mysteriously at New Street Station.

Mike breathed a sigh of relief, of course he was now wanted for murder but thought he had covered his tracks well and felt the pressure was now off. He went back to his family and had a real family weekend, taking the children and Debbie out and feeling like the threat hanging over his for the last few days had now gone away.

Chapter 12 – It's in the Paper

Guildford, October 2019

As it turned out he was very wrong. Two weeks after the demise of Karl, Andy sent him an article from the Manchester Evening News:

<u>What happened to Warrington's Dave Lawrence – is he still alive?</u>

Dave Lawrence was a high-flying banker from Warrington who went to New York on secondment in the late 1990s. It was assumed that he had died in the Twin Towers Terrorist attack of 9/11 as he worked in his office in the South Tower of the World Trade Centre.

We have received an anonymous letter stating that he now lives in England under an assumed name of Mike Stead.

Do you know Mike Stead? If so, please contact us on 0116 345 6734 or email us on scoops@men.co.uk

Mike was at his desk in the office, and he immediately felt sick. His body almost shook as he read about himself – the reality of who he was, who he is, and that people are now onto him. He spent nearly as much money buying the poison that killed Karl as it would have been to pay him off – is he in any better position now? Karl was evil that's for sure and no doubt he would have come back again having sown the first seed in the newspaper. Bizarrely Mike thought it good that the article was anonymous otherwise that thread would now lead to a dead man and make the hunt for Mike more intensive.

Nevertheless, there would now be a hunt to search him out. How long did he have left before his past caught up with him? Does he need to tell Debbie? Does he need a plan B (again)?

In fact, one thing he had learned from his previous experience was that you need money, whatever happens. He decided to leverage as much cash as possible without alerting his bank, business and family too much. He arranged more credit cards even though he had £120,000 limits with no current borrowing. He withdrew £50k from his business and £25k from his personal saving account in cash, plus drew around half of the cash available on his credit cards. He therefore now has around £150k in a suitcase and could access around another £100k if he needed to do it. He had already created two alternative identities several years ago in a moment of panic when he thought about what would happen if anyone found out. He had not chosen former friends as his alternative identities this time, but two other children who had died young where he obtained their birth certificates and built a 'legend.' He also rented a lock up in Portsmouth, which he used as the address for his fake identities. He visited every three months or so to check on the place, unknown to Debbie.

He really didn't know what was in store for him, but he held back from giving Debbie the shock of her life. Maybe it would go away, the fact that it was in a regional paper and there must be thousands of Mike Steads around the country.

Chapter 13 – Luck of the Irish

Guildford, October 2019

Mike was at his desk a week or so later, concentrating on a deal he was working on for a Manufacturing firm, rolling up a series of acquisitions when he was conscious of a tall man standing in front of him. He was instantly nervous after the last time this happened.

"Can I help you sir," asked Mike

You certainly can Mr Stead my boss would like to talk to you about a business proposition. Let me get him on the phone, "I'm Dermot by the way," and they shook hands before Dermot dialled a number and sat down.

Without further thought, Mike took the phone, thinking it may be a business deal only to be shocked by the next words he heard: "Hello, Dave, it's Ger here from New York how are you my old friend?" Mike crumbled; he knew he was in trouble.

"There is the small matter of one hundred thousand dollars… plus, interest. Dermot there will show you how much the interest is and how much you need to pay us back son."

Dermot handed over a piece of paper with the original sum less one payment made plus interest over eighteen years. The total amount was $745,079 dollars.

"Sure, and we can let you off the seventy-nine dollars Dave me old pal. Just make sure Dermot gets the money in the next seven days or we will be taking other assets of yours" Ger hung up with the threat hanging in the air.

"I haven't got that sort of money Dermot," said Mike.

"We don't care about that Mike, if you rip our company off like you have done there is no end to what we will do to get this money back. It's cash within seven days, your house, your business – or your family," now give me your hand, and within a second he had snapped a thick cord around Mike's wrist, "that's a tracker so we will know where you are, we are not letting you get away this time. We are also keeping an eye on your family so don't try anything silly."

With that Dermot walked out and Mike sat there in silence staring at the wall – a small piece of wallpaper that was crumbling in the corner. He sat there for thirty minutes before he left the office and went for a long walk down by the river Wey.

Mike sat on a bench by the river, his phone switched off and his whole body was aching with the stress of now knowing he had to pay back the Irish Americans. He believed that they will not mess around, and he knows something has to give. He has his 'stash' and his credit cards, but they were his emergency fund 'just in case' and who knows where all this leads? He has started to pick up on the mention of his family not just the money. What might they do to Debbie and the kids? Was it a bluff? He decided he couldn't take the chance. He was going to have to talk to Debbie and tell them the mess they were now in – it won't be pleasant!

Chapter 14 – A Time to Tell

Mike told Debbie that tonight they needed to get away from the house, just the two of them and that there was something urgent to talk about. He booked a room at the Runnymede Hotel, Egham so that they could go and talk together in peace and away from the kids and the neighbours.

Mike didn't even drive with Debbie, he went on ahead and met her there which she thought odd. She started to wonder what this was about – has Mike got someone else? She couldn't bear to be without him he was the centre of her world. She could forgive him for anything, but she is not sure about forgiving an affair.

Debbie arrived at the hotel and went straight to room 361 where Mike was waiting, sat on the edge of the bed.

"What's the matter Mike," she said as she saw Mike, ashen faced.

"I've got something really big to tell you love and it is going to rock your world. I am really sorry, but I must tell you as I think we both might be in danger."

Mike told his 'back story' – the one prior to landing back in the UK and prior to meeting her. She had subconsciously realised that Mike had left big gaps in his history but accepted it as him and never really questioned it. He had previously told her that he had been to New York with the bank he worked for previously but not about his secondment there.

Mike explained about getting into debt – although he missed out the part about Melissa – he couldn't face telling Debbie that there had been someone else. He told her all about the false identity, the money he borrowed from Shamrock, the day of the twin towers attack and his few days locked away before his across America trip and eventual return.

Debbie of course was truly shocked. She couldn't understand how he had got into such debt, which didn't seem to be in his nature, and she had never seen that side of him in their years together. She was shocked about the use of his dead friend as an alias and her instant reaction was to want to call him Dave instead of Mike.

But of course, the real burning issue is the money owed now to the loan shark side of the Shamrock organisation. How are they going to pay back hundreds of thousands of dollars?

The conversation went on pretty much all night and the emotions swung from despair to anger to sadness and almost complete desperation.

Eventually as four a.m. came around they were both agreed that it was one of two solutions – either they hand over the business (it was making around £350k profit per year so this would be fair value) or they hand over their house (which would sell for around £1.5m and had a £650,000 mortgage on it).

He had Ger's number on his phone and called him even though it was midnight in New York.

Ger picked up immediately. "Ger – it's Mike… er Dave Lawrence. Listen I fully accept that I owe you the money, I am very sorry that I never paid you back, but I will do the right thing now." He explained the two options that they had come up with and asked Ger what they would propose as they were unable to raise the £650,000 cash.

"We'll take the business Dave, we like legit businesses which are making a profit, they can be very useful for us. You can stay and run it and to the world at large it looks the same, but you will report to me and follow instructions – OK?" Mike was slightly relieved, said yes and agreed to sign the paperwork in two days' time on Friday morning when Dermot would bring the papers.

Debbie put her arms around him and cried. "At least it's not the end of everything for us we can still live in the house, and you can still do the same work which I know you love – you will just have a new boss."

They slept for an hour and then the following morning went back home satisfied they were over the worst.

Chapter 15 – Money Laundering

December 2019

Mike now understood why they wanted the business, their plan was to launder bad money through the good, profitable and respectable business. He was still getting paid; he was still doing his job, but he was now a front for an Irish American crime gang that would hang him out to dry at any moment if they needed to. He knew he was living on a knife edge and his nerves jangled. However, he felt the wolf had been sent from the door and they could at least carry-on living – his worst fears perhaps have not come to pass.

They had a fairly quiet Christmas, enjoyable, just the family and all spent at home. Debbie and Mike appreciated the time they had together and the fact that the pressure seemed like it was off.

That was until New Year's Eve around mid-day when there was a ring on the bell. Mike answered it, opened the door and to his utter horror saw another face from the past. She was older, a little greyer and a shade heavier but Melissa still had that mischievous look in her eye. "Hello husband how are you, have you bought me a Christmas present?" she said without much humour. Mike tried to get out of the door to see her on his own, but first Harvey pushed through with a playful bark and then Louisa pushed the door open further "who's this dad?", Debbie followed her out a few seconds later.

"You had better come in," said Mike, utterly dejected as he knew the storm that was about to break.

It could be described as all hell let loose. Melissa didn't make it easy and was as provocative as she could possibly have been, talking about her husband, how he left her with lots of debts, how he ran away from her, has not been in touch for nearly twenty years and how she has pined after him. She had pointed out within minutes how ½ the house belonged to her as his wife!

Debbie was angry at first shouting at Melissa, but as the news sunk in, she realised the shocking truth – that Mike was a bigamist. He was still married to Melissa and therefore their whole life had been a lie. She started hitting Mike and raging at him until Kenny stopped her and said, "Let's listen to what Dad has to say."

But there was nothing to say that wasn't the truth. He was married to Melissa, he faked his death, started a new life, has lost his business and is now a criminal (and also a murderer!) operating for a crime gang and moreover his marriage to Debbie is a sham. Melissa being Melissa would take them for every penny.

Melissa left around three p.m. after what was for all of them, probably the worst day of their lives. Happy New Year didn't seem to be a good message at that moment either between them all or on the TV which they switched off.

"I hate you Mike, how could you do this to me, to us? We have lost everything, and it has all been a lie. How did you think you would get away with this? You need to leave now, it's all over between us and I need to fight for what's mine now," said Debbie.

Mike understood, he had nothing to argue with and he went and packed a suitcase. He also picked up his emergency suitcase from the high cupboard in the wardrobe which Debbie would never have been able to reach.

He left as they were all crying including him, walking down the drive, tears in his eyes getting into his big black car which now seemed so inappropriate.

He stopped in a layby 2 miles away, firstly to check he had not been followed and second to look on Booking.com to find somewhere to stay. He decided he needed to hide from everyone until he could work out what to do for the best, so he booked into a Central London hotel from a burner phone in his suitcase and with a credit card in the name of Andrew Myers. Andrew Myers was a boy who died aged four in 1982. Little did his parents know his alter ego was now a wanted criminal.

'Andrew' left his car at Gatwick airport long stay as a misdirection for those that would now be looking for him (the police for example – as a bigamist). He struggled to get the wristband off but with the help of his toolkit which he kept in the back of the car he managed to do it, although he cut himself badly on the hand in the process. He took the wristband into the airport and flushed it down a toilet. He got on the train into London before the new year celebrations got under way and tried to stay as anonymous as possible.

He checked into the Marlin 4* hotel near Waterloo and relaxed on his bed. What a dire situation, he couldn't believe how all the dominoes had fallen one by one and so quickly. He has lost his house and business, lost his wife and children, gained an ex-wife he never thought he would see again, and he was on the run as a bigamist. He had no choice now but to go on the run and start a new life. He would find it hard without his lovely family who he adored but prison or torture was not something he was prepared to endure.

Then something truly shocking happened – on New Year's night as revellers danced, smiled and kissed and Big Ben struck twelve p.m. Midnight there was the most almighty BOOM.

He looked out of the window and saw a massive flume of flames coming from near the river. He switched on the TV and the reporters were saying there has been a huge terrorist attack, a bomb had gone off under the London Eye and it was devastation. *"I've been here before,"* he thought and quick thinking, took his Mike Stead passport with him and set off towards the flames.

He arrived a few minutes later and whilst police were trying to build a cordon around it there were chaotic scenes, people everywhere, bodies burned, flames flying through the sky and the sound of screams everywhere. Utter horror – even worse than he remembered at 9/11.

Mike ran as close to the centre of the scene as possible, took off his jacket and laid it on top of a burned body. His 'Mike' passport was in the pocket, and he mentally said goodbye to his old self (again). History is repeating itself and once again he has the world at his feet and a new adventure ahead.